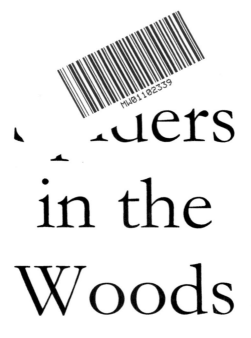

Murders in the Woods

Lorraine Kean

PublishAmerica
Baltimore

First printing

ISBN: 1-59129-580-7
PUBLISHED BY
PUBLISHAMERICA BOOK PUBLISHERS
www.publishamerica.com
Baltimore

Printed in the United States of America

This book is dedicated to my husband Jim, my helpmate.

Acknowledgements

Thank you to my granddaughter Jessica, for being my best critic, and to Kim, who provided me with her honest and most valuable input to the writing of this book

Chapter One
The Discovery

"Wow! Did you see that?" said Bob.

My cousin Bob and I were staring out of his bedroom window in the upper floor of his house. We were supposed to be doing our homework, but instead we were gazing at the darkening sky, which was quickly filling with twinkling stars. "Yeah," I answered. "What do you think it was?"

Bob, who was the smarter of the two of us, thought for a moment. "Maybe it is a comet or a meteor or, jeez, I don't know. Tomorrow is Saturday," he continued with a strange look in his eye. "Let's go and see if it landed on the other side of the island. Maybe we can find it."

"No, you are not going to involve me in one of your wild goose chases again," I said, and gathered up my books and jacket. There was no doubt that I would go with him. Nothing could stop me! Bob knew that I would be just as excited about looking for a meteorite as he was.

"You got us into a lot of trouble with your last stunt!" I complained. I was talking about the mess he got us into when he thought that Mr. Robbins down the street had robbed the bank. But that's another story.

"Don't you have any sense of adventure?" he shouted as I ran down the stairs.

Grade six boys! They were all a bunch of thrill seekers.

I found my way through the dark hallway into the kitchen, where my aunt was seated at the table, doing a crossword puzzle. "Good night, Aunt Margie," I said and walked past her.

"Good night, dear," she replied absently, not looking up, obviously very interested in what she was doing.

The drone of the TV set was coming from the den. No doubt Uncle Tim and my rotten little cousin Billy were watching the tube. Someone could have walked away with the family jewels and not one of them would have noticed.

"Did you get your homework done, dear?" inquired Mom as I came in the front door. "Some of it," I replied carefully, and flopped into the easy chair. We actually hadn't done any at all between gabbing and staring at the stars.

"The end of the school year is not far off, you'd better keep up," she cautioned.

"I know that, Mom, but my grades are pretty good," I said.

Our house was very small. We had to move after Dad left, because Mom didn't make a lot of money. When Dad was with us, we lived in a big house with windows looking out over the ocean. It had been over a year since he went away, and I really missed him. We hadn't heard a word from him in all that time. It was just as if he had disappeared from the face of the earth. Dad was an artist. That was one of the reasons we had moved to the island. The island was home to a lot of painters.

Mom looked so tired tonight. Her job at the real estate office kept her very busy, and she often worked late. We really had a struggle to make ends meet. I didn't care, as long as Mom and I were together. She was so gentle, loving and kind.

"It's time for you to go bed, Jess," Mom said. "Will you wake me up early tomorrow, Mom?" I asked. "Bob and I are going over to the other side of the island. We thought we saw a meteorite fall over that way. We are going to check it out."

"Ok, dear," Mom replied, "but remember, you have to help me with the housework and the laundry."

"Is it all right if we do it when we get back?" I asked hopefully.

Mom smiled her beautiful smile and answered, "Yes, but don't be gone past lunch time."

"Oh we'll be back by then," I called over my shoulder and headed for my room. "Night, Mom, sleep well." I turned around and blew her a kiss. She did the same.

In my room, I stared at myself in the mirror. Ugh! My hair looked like it usually did, just like a fuzz ball. Mom kept my dark blond hair cut real short because it was so wild and curly. I really hated my hair. How wonderful it would be to have smooth straight hair like some of the models you see on TV advertising shampoo. It got combed once a day, but hardly ever more than that, because that didn't make any difference. It always looked as though a tornado had run through it.

I was small for my age. That was ok, as long as nobody called me Shorty. Dad used to call me Shorty, which was his nickname for me. I didn't mind when he called me that, but no one else could. They would have a fight on their hands if they did. I rolled my little hands into fists just thinking about it.

My eyes were green, same as my mom's. She was pretty. It would be nice to grow up to look just like her. She was tall though. Little Jess must have inherited genes from some short person in the family.

I slept really well and woke the next morning to the sound of the doorbell. My watch said eight o'clock, wow! I really did zonk out! I got up, threw on my robe, and went to the door. Mom must have forgotten to wake me.

It was Bob, all set to go. He even had his backpack with him.

"What's in that?" I asked, and poked at it a couple of times.

"A sandwich and a pop in case I get hungry," was his answer.

"Remember, I have to be home by noon to help Mom with the work around here," I warned him. "And by the way, how did you sneak out on that pesky little brother of yours?"

"He was still asleep. He and Dad watched TV until late," Bob replied. Bob looked mysterious. "There was nothing on the news about our meteorite," he said, "so it might be all ours."

I just looked at him and sighed.

"Hurry up and get dressed," urged Bob. "We have to get going."

"Ok, ok. What's the big rush?" I grouched.

I ran to my room. I pulled on my jeans, T-shirt, and runners, then I quickly dragged a comb through my hair. My curls kept getting tangled. It pulled like crazy. "Darn this hair any way," I shouted and ran out the door.

"Ready, are we, at last?" Bob asked.

"Don't be so smart," I snarled.

"Is there a sandwich and pop in there for me?" I inquired, pointing to the backpack. "Of course," he said with a laugh "I knew you wouldn't be ready, so I took the time to make yours."

I punched him on the shoulder and said, "You know, for a boy and a relative, you're not half bad."

"Thanks, I think," was his answer. His face looked a little red.

Bob was kind of a geeky-looking guy, who was awfully tall and a little skinny. I knew that one day he would probably look really great. He towered over me by several inches, even though we were the same age. His hair was dark brown.

There was always a piece of it falling over his glasses, which were as thick as coke bottles. He said he was nearsighted.

Bob was really smart though. He was a straight A student. I was a B or B+ person. I felt a little jealous, because he found school so easy. I always had to work so hard. It didn't seem fair.

"Ok, let's go," I said, and flung my light jacket over the bicycle carrier. "It looks like rain." It seemed like it rained a lot on the island; in fact, rain was pretty much normal.

"I didn't bring mine," Bob declared. "It's going to be sunny."

Suddenly, I remembered. Mom went out grocery shopping, better leave her a note. I ran back and scribbled a quick note, saying we would be back by noon, then we took off.

The other side of the island wasn't very far. Our little island was quite narrow. "What makes you think it landed here at all?" I asked Bob as we started out.

"Just a guess," he answered.

We hadn't gone any more than a couple of kilometers when it started to rain. Not heavy, just that kind of West Coast drizzle. I stopped and put on my hooded windbreaker. Bob hunched his shoulders, blinking as the moisture sort of oozed down his face. "See, I told you that you should have brought some rain gear," I said.

"Well, it's too late now," he snorted, and sped up the pace.

By the time we got to where we thought the meteorite had landed, the rain had stopped. The sun was peeking out from behind the clouds. We parked our bikes and started looking around.

"I don't see a thing. This is a waste of time." I complained.

"Be patient! Be patient!" Bob scolded as he continued to prowl through the bushes and disturb every spider that lived there. Yikes, how I hated spiders! I would rather jump off a cliff than be covered in those creepy crawlies.

Finally, we came to a clearing, and Bob started to run. He yelled, "I think I see something," pointing to a dark-looking thing about thirty meters away.

"It's probably just another old rock."

Bob looked at me over his glasses and said in a nagging voice, "The problem with you is that you have no imagination and no sense of adventure."

"I have too," I snorted. "Didn't I write that story about the pirates that Mrs. Wilde, our grade five teacher, thought was so good? She even read it to the whole class."

"Well, maybe you did write a good story, but that doesn't mean much when it comes to exploring for lost meteorites," was his smart reply.

We approached the thing that looked like a very dark-coloured rock. When we got closer, we could tell that it was different all right. It was about a meter long and kind of egg-shaped. We guessed that it was about half a meter wide. It was unusual-looking and had kind of a rough, bumpy surface. It seemed to change colors ever so slightly, or could it be glowing? Freaky! I started to get a little interested, 'cause it did look very odd. I picked up a stick and started to poke at the thing. Little dents appeared in the spots where the stick had poked.

Bob put his finger in the little dents. He looked puzzled, but all he said was, "Cool, isn't it?" The more he studied it, the more excited Bob seemed to become. He started dancing around the thing like it was the most wonderful piece of rock he had ever seen. "It looks like it could be a meteorite, but if it is, it sure is a different one," he said.

"Well, now that we've seen it, can we go?" I nagged.

LORRAINE KEAN

"Of course we can go," he replied. "I just wanted to see for myself. But you know, it is a strange sort of rock," Bob continued. "You saw how soft it was. Maybe we should come back to look at it again."

"Do you expect it to suddenly sprout wings and start flying?" I teased.

"Let's just come back tomorrow and have another look," Bob coaxed as he hopped on his bike, ready to leave.

"Hey, how about eating those sandwiches," I asked. "I worked up an appetite riding out here. Remember, we didn't have any breakfast."

"It was you that didn't have breakfast, I did," Bob reminded me

We sat in the grass, ate peanut butter and jelly sandwiches, and talked about where the old hunk of boulder might have come from. The sun was shining and the birds were singing. It had turned out to be a great day after all

Feeling kind of dozy, I stood up, yawned and announced, "It's almost noon. I have to get back home to help Mom."

"Yeah, I promised to help Dad mow the lawn if the weather was good, so we better get going, but we are coming back tomorrow, right?" Bob demanded.

"Ok," I agreed. "I guess there isn't anything more important to do."

We rode back in silence. When we got close to my house, Bob looked serious as he said, "Don't tell a soul about this or there will be dozens of people out in the woods looking at our rock. Maybe they might even take it away."

"I won't," I promised. "You aren't going to tell that nosy little brother of yours are you?"

"Of course not," he snickered. "What do you think I am, crazy? He blabs everything he hears to anyone who will listen."

It was exactly twelve when I leapt off my bike in our driveway. Mom was waiting at the front door. "Well, did you find anything?" she asked.

I shrugged my shoulders and said, "Not much, are you ready to get at the work?"

"Right now," she answered enthusiastically.

Thoughts about the meteorite we had seen went through my mind as I helped with the housework. Going back out to the other side of the island was a really cool idea! Maybe the meteorite would be different. That would really be neat!

About three thirty, as we sat in the front room, work all done, Mom said, "Well, everything is finished, how about a treat at the ice cream store?"

"You don't have to ask me twice," was my reply. I was out of the chair and at the door in two seconds.

After we had pigged out on Chocolate Cherry Delight, Mom asked, "Would you like to rent a movie tonight or would you like to go over to the big island to see that new movie that is playing?"

"How about we rent tonight? You made me work so hard I am too tired to get ready to go out," I joked.

"Fine with me," Mom answered, "cheaper too."

We rented a couple of videos, watched them and ate microwave popcorn. The movies weren't very good. I fell asleep in the middle of the second one.

All evening I had been thinking about that meteorite. I didn't know why, but it was on my mind.

Bob phoned about nine o'clock to remind me that we had to go back to the other side of the island in the morning.

At ten, we shut the TV off and went to bed, but I couldn't sleep. My mind was working overtime. What would we find the next day? The thing that had fallen on the island was pretty cool. I hoped no one else would find it and spoil our fun.

I tossed and turned for ages, finally falling asleep. I didn't dream though. I guess I was too tired.

Chapter Two
The Egg

The next day, Mom and I got up early and went to the church service at ten.

After that, I rushed home to change and was ready to go when Bob showed up with his backpack full of sandwiches, cookies and juice. "I am going to have to start paying you for these lunches," I joked as we took off on our bikes.

It was a perfect day. The air smelled like pine and fresh cut grass. We hadn't gone very far when I felt like we were not alone. I looked over my shoulder but couldn't see anyone. Oh well, I must be a little freaked out, I thought.

We got to the spot where the meteorite had landed. It was in exactly the same place it had been the day before. "Good! No one has been here," Bob said.

Just then, we heard a rustle in the trees and who should walk out but little Billy.

"What are you doing here?" I asked.

He looked kind of guilty and answered, "I

saw you two acting kind of weird, and I listened to the conversation you had on the phone last night. I decided to follow you to see what was going on. If you don't let me in on this, I will tell every one that you two are up to some thing really creepy."

"You are being a pain," Bob scolded. "You know you are not supposed to listen in on other people's phone conversations. Dad would be really mad if he knew."

"You won't tell him, will you?" begged Billy. "He would ground me for a month."

"I guess not. If we show you what we've found, you must promise not to tell a soul, on pain of death!" his brother demanded.

"I promise," Billy said very solemnly.

Bob showed Billy the meteorite.

"Wow! Where do you think it came from?" said Billy.

"We don't know, but it came down on Friday night. So far, you, Jess, and I are the only ones who know about it. If too many people find out, it won't be our secret anymore. The whole world will know," Bob answered.

We walked around the rock a couple of times. Bob was insisting that it looked very different. It did look like it was vibrating or throbbing in a strange way, and the color seemed to be changing from black to dark green, to dark gray. Then it would start all over again. I blinked a couple of times to make sure I wasn't seeing things. Wow! It was so spooky! It was almost like it was alive.

Bob touched it but quickly pulled his hand away like it had been burned. "Yikes! It feels almost spongy and softer than a rock should feel. Sure is different all right. Jess, come over here and touch it. Tell me what you think," he said.

"It makes me feel really weird. Do I have to?" I asked

"Maybe we should tell someone about it," I said.

"I don't want to do that, at least not yet," Bob exclaimed. "Let's study it for a while to see what happens. It could be that we are just imagining that it is changing. After all, it is just a rock, isn't it?" He sounded awfully unsure.

Billy was just standing there with his mouth open. He wasn't saying a word.

Finally, I walked over and touched the rock, then, jumped back startled. "There is no doubt about it, it is different than it was yesterday. Do you remember the pet Python that Patrick used to have? The one that escaped and was never found? Well, it feels like that, sort of cool, but leathery and soft," I said. "And look, it really does change color! I don't know what it is, but it is spooky."

At last, Billy closed his mouth and said, "Maybe we should tell Mom and Dad. They would know what to do."

"We are going to wait for a while. There's lots of time to tell them if we need to," Bob answered.

We hung around the thing for a little while, watching it. Nothing happened, except that you could see it continue to pulsate ever so slightly. Everything else in the little stretch of woods looked the same. I had an eerie feeling. It was worse than the feeling I got when creepy spiders were around.

"Let's go down to the beach and eat our lunch," Bob suggested.

"Did you bring enough for me?" inquired Billy.

"Well, I guess so, but you weren't invited, so don't expect too much. However, Jess and I will share," Bob replied.

We ate our lunch without talking. I guessed that each of us had his own thoughts about the thing that was lying a few meters away. My brain told me we should tell someone, but I had given my word to Bob.

As we rode home, Bob suggested that after school tomorrow we have another look at the thing.

"Me too!" Billy piped up.

"I think we better keep an eye on it. I have a bad feeling about this," I said, ignoring Billy.

"I wish I knew more about meteorites and stuff like that. I know a little, but not enough. I am going to the library to read more about them," Bob said.

Mom was reading a book when I got home. "Where were you, dear?" she asked.

"Oh, Bob and I were just riding our bikes around and hanging out," came my answer. I was pleased with myself for doing such a good job of keeping our secret.

"It's after two. Did you have lunch?" Mom asked.

"Yes, Bob brought some sandwiches and juice."

Mom was making a great supper of fried chicken with baked potatoes. She told me that our neighbour, Ms. Inglis, was invited for supper. Ms. I. was a librarian and was probably really intelligent, but I thought she was strange.

She always wore a head-band and the same old clothes. She spoke in sentences of one word. It seemed really hard to have a conversation with her. Mom said she was just shy, so I suppose that explained why she talked so little.

After dinner, we sat around, chitchatting with Ms. Inglis. Mom did most of the talking. Ms. Inglis did most of the listening. Finally she decided to go home. Boy, was I ever glad, 'cause I wanted to watch TV for a while before I had to go to bed.

I phoned Bob and reminded him to warn his little brother about not blabbing. He told me not to worry, that he had figured out a way to keep Billy quiet.

Bob wanted to know for sure if I was going with him tomorrow. I was good to go and anxious to see if the thing had changed overnight.

School went fine the next day, except that I had forgotten to do my math homework. In all the excitement over the weekend, it had slipped my mind completely. Somehow, Bob had remembered to do his. This did not make me feel any better.

After school, I had to go home to do some chores. I rushed through the jobs, then went over to Bob's house to wait for him.

I played with Taffy, his pet Cocker Spaniel. Taffy was full of fun, always ready to play ball. After we were both nearly exhausted, Bob came around the corner.

"Where were you?" I asked, "this dog has worn me out. He never seems to get tired of playing ball."

"I decided to go to the library to find out more about meteorites but didn't learn any thing new," was his answer.

"Let's get going," I said. Do you think we can get out of here before Billy sees us?"

Just then Billy showed his face through the front door and asked when we were going. "Can we take Taffy?" he asked.

"No," Bob replied. "He might bark at the thing and draw attention to it. You know it's just outside the park. I am surprised that someone else hasn't seen it by now."

We took off on our bikes. Mom was still at work. I was sure glad that we didn't have to tell her that we were taking off again. She would have been suspicious. "We have to be back by five, because supper has to be started," I warned them.

It was a cloudy, miserable day. No one said a

word as we rode out to the woods. I was feeling really anxious about the thing hidden in the trees. Did I really want to see what was happening? On the other hand, it was kind of exciting.

When we were inside the woods, I pulled my jacket tight around me and zipped up. It was cold, but after all, it was only the middle of April. Bob ran over to the meteorite, I dragged my feet, and Billy hung back.

"It hasn't changed," Bob said. He looked really disappointed. "I still think we should come here every day until we are sure nothing more is going to happen to it." He turned away, ready to leave.

"But it has changed!" I shouted. "Come, look over here at this side. There is a small crack in the thing!"

In my excitement, I tripped over a tree root, falling flat on my face. "Ouch, that hurt!" I yelled.

Bob and Billy ignored me completely, because they were looking at the crack in the side of the meteorite.

"You're right," Bob said. "Look at that. But maybe it was here before and we didn't notice. Oops, sorry, Jess. Did you get hurt?"

"Oh no, nothing that a cast and a pair of crutches won't fix," I replied in my most offended manner.

"Let me help you up," Bob offered.

"No, I am ok," I said, managing to get up and brush the dirt off. "That crack wasn't there before, believe me," I told him.

"This is really weird. I can't understand how an ordinary meteorite would change like this. What do you make of it, Jess? Bob asked. "Gee I don't have a clue," I replied. "I know we can't stay here to baby-sit this thing. We have to go home. Our parents are expecting us for dinner."

"Do you think we could come back again tomorrow?" Bob asked.

"Tomorrow is Mom's birthday. We are going out for hamburgers and milk shakes," I answered.

"I just remembered, the guys want me to play softball with them after school, so I can't come out either," Bob said.

"Well, we will just have to leave it and come back as soon as we can," I said.

We picked up a few branches that were lying on the ground and put them around the thing to keep it hidden from sight as much as possible.

I had made a cute card on the computer for Mom and managed to save enough from my allowance to buy her some nice bath soap. What was left would take us to the Burger Barn.

Mom hummed softly as we walked to the restaurant Tuesday evening. She seemed happy enough, but I wished she wasn't so lonely. Maybe she isn't lonely, I thought. After all, she has me!

When we got home, I asked Mom if she still missed Dad as much as I did. Her face sort of crumpled, and tears rolled down her cheeks. Finally she answered me. "Yes, Jess, I do, but he made a choice that did not include us. We really have to face the fact that we are probably better off this way."

"I am sorry I mentioned it, Mom, but sometimes it helps me to talk about it," I said.

"That makes two of us, sweetie," she answered. "I have you, and that is what is important. Thanks so much for the nice birthday." She managed a smile and gave me a hug.

The next day at school, I talked to Bob about going back out to see the thing in the woods. We decided to go right after school. Maybe we could give Billy the slip. No such luck! When Bob came by my house, there was Billy the pest with him.

It was raining, and I didn't really feel like going outside, but I was so curious, I had to find out what was going on with the thing.

When we got near the meteorite, Bob was pedaling his bike so fast he almost upset before he got it stopped.

The egg-like thing was still pulsating very slightly, but it looked like it had shrunk somehow. Sort of like it was wrinkling up and imploding slowly. We walked around and around it. We were all trying to figure out what was happening.

Suddenly I started to scream. "Oh, gross, this is so gross!"

There was a sticky gooey brown liquid coming out of the split in the egg. In this stuff, there were black things that looked like insects. They were very small, about the size of teeny flies, and were struggling to free themselves from the goo. Bob looked at the mess and shook his head. "This isn't any ordinary meteorite, that's for sure."

"Do you suppose it came here for some particular reason?" Bob said.

I looked at him, unable to believe what he had just said. "What do you mean? Are you saying that some alien beings sent this here deliberately?"

"That is exactly what I am saying," said Bob.

"But why would they do that? What could be their reason?" I asked.

"That, we don't know," he answered. "But we'd better watch it closely. Maybe I am all wrong, probably it is just some huge egg sac made by some kind of insect."

We had to leave, because it was getting close to five o'clock. It was time to get home. On the way, thoughts about the ooky syrupy stuff with the insects stuck in it kept turning around in my head. I shivered. Why did I feel like this? It was likely just some ordinary everyday bug that we hadn't seen hatching before. Somehow, I didn't think so. It was creepy all right.

When I got home, Mom was already there. She had started to peel the potatoes.

"That's my job," I said, feeling mean because I had not been home in time to get the meal started.

Mom was kind of cross, but she didn't say much. She looked like she was not pleased, as her brow was all furrowed and she had that you-are-a-very-naughty-girl-look on her face. She also looked worried. I decided to leave well enough alone and went to work getting the other vegetables ready without saying another word.

We ate our supper without speaking. Something is wrong, I thought. It was not like Mom to be so quiet, even when she is put off with me

After we finished our meal, I said, "I'll clean up. You go and rest."

"Thanks," she murmured, and disappeared into the living room.

When the dishes were done, I went in to the living too. Mom was sitting on the sofa. She looked up and said "Mr. Green, my boss at work, says he is going to have to lay someone off if business doesn't improve. Since there are only two of us in the office and the junior person is the one to go, it will be me."

"Oh, Mom, I am sorry," I said, "but things will get better. They always do in the summer." I tried to reassure her, but didn't feel too sure that it was helping.

"I hope you are right, dear," was her reply.

Oh great! Now this is something else for me to worry about, I thought. As if the bugs on the other side of the island weren't enough!

I didn't sleep well. All I dreamed about was bugs crawling all over everything including me. I woke up at six a.m., got up, went to the kitchen, and poured myself a glass of juice, then turned on the TV real low so it wouldn't wake Mom up. I had to watch the early morning news. That was about all that was on.

Finally, it was time to get ready for school. I dragged myself back to my room, had a shower, and got dressed for school.

It was raining hard. My hair got all frizzed up on the way to school. Oh bother, what's the use anyway!

Bob was waiting for me. He looked kind of worried as he dragged me into a corner and whispered, "We are going out to look at the bugs again after school. You can't refuse. I don't care if it is raining cats and dogs out there."

"Ok, ok," I said. "Don't get so excited." I told him we would meet at the strange egg at three o'clock.

I was anxious all that day about what would be new and different with our bugs and what we would find when we got to the woods.

As soon as school got out, I rushed home, changed and took off for the other side of the island. Bob was already there. He didn't have the pest with him.

"Look," Bob bellowed "These things are out of the muck, and it seems to have all dried up. The little creatures look larger than they did yesterday."

They were moving around, all very active. One of them crawled over my shoe. I bent down really close to it and said, "Hi, little bug." Suddenly, a black antenna shot up out of its head. It was almost as if it had understood me. Impossible, I reasoned. My imagination has gone crazy today!

Bob saw it too and said, "It heard you, Jess."

I wanted to get away from there, go home and never come back. It was just so weird. I stayed though, because my curiosity was greater than my fear.

Chapter Three
Meet Professor Ipswich

"Maybe we can catch one to take to my friend Professor Ipswich," suggested Bob. He got down on his hands and knees, looking really closely at the little bugs.

When he got up, he said, "They look like spiders. You can count eight legs. But they also have antennae. I have never seen a spider like this before."

The little things were crawling about in circles. They acted like they were lost.

"Spiders! I am getting out of here," I announced. With that, I jumped on my bike, ready to take off for home.

Bob caught up with me and said, "What's the matter with you? You said we were going to stay together on this."

"The whole thing has got me scared. You know how I feel about spiders, Bob. They make me freak out. They are so creepy. Besides, we should tell someone about them."

"Ok, I will go and talk to my friend the professor. Perhaps he can help. Will that satisfy you?" asked Bob.

"Sure, that's a good idea. Is he really smart? People say that he is very odd," I said.

When I got home, Mom wasn't there yet. It was still my job to start the meal. Mom and I had made a deal about this.

After supper, Bob phoned to tell me that we could go to see the professor at three thirty the next day.

Mom looked really tired again. After we had cleaned up the kitchen, she asked if we could go into the living room, because she wanted to talk to me about something. We both sat down. She looked at me sadly and said, "I received a registered letter from your Dad today. He is in some little place in California. He says he is not coming back. He is filing for divorce. The papers should be here any day now. He sent a separate letter for you. Here it is." She handed me a thin white envelope. I took it from her but felt like I was having a bad dream, that none of this was real. I couldn't believe it. No word for almost a year and now this!

I read the short letter. All it said was that he loved me very much, but he was happy in

California. He didn't want to come back to the island. The letter went on to say that Mom and I were better off without him. He hoped I would understand. Understand! I couldn't begin to! I couldn't believe this was happening

After reading the note, I just sat there until Mom finally spoke. She said, "Jess, we now know for sure that your dad is not coming back. We must put the past behind us and go on. There is no point in us trying to wish for something that can never be. I know how unhappy you are, but there isn't much that either of us can do about it. At least you know that he is ok."

"You are right, Mom, what you say is true. I think I will go to my room now and read for a while," I said. Flopping on my bed, I started to cry in to my pillow, finally falling asleep.

I woke up the next morning, feeling a bit better. Mom didn't mention it again. It was a beautiful sunny day. She had cooked pancakes and eggs, and had put a pretty little bouquet of flowers on the dining room table.

After breakfast, I left for school in a happier mood. It was the last day of the week. The weekend was coming! Not that I didn't like school, it was all right, but the weekends were better.

I now knew where my dad was and that nothing terrible had happened to him. That made me feel a tiny bit ok about all this. I was angry with him for leaving us, but maybe it was my fault. If I had been a more perfect daughter, he wouldn't have gone away. It made me so sad.

Then I remembered the bugs, and the scared feeling came again. Something told me that they were very unusual, that we should be doing something about them other than just visiting them every day.

I had trouble concentrating in school that day. Ms. Bowman asked me a question. I didn't even hear her. Annoyed, she repeated it, and I didn't know the answer. She told me to pay more attention in class and stop daydreaming. Every one in the room was looking at me. My face felt like it was on fire.

After school, my friend Marcie came over to talk to me. She said I looked upset. I told her about the letter from my dad and because of that I hadn't slept much last night. I didn't tell her about what Bob and I had found in the bushes on the other side of the island. She would probably think that both Bob and I were crazy.

She wanted to walk home with me, but I told her they were waiting at the dentist's office for me.

Bob met me at the corner store. We biked to Professor Ipswich's home, which was fairly close to Bob's. The house was lost behind a thick growth of trees and bushes. Bob opened the rusty gate, and we went inside the yard. We saw that everything was so overgrown with grass and weeds you could hardly find the door. Bob knocked several times before the door was answered.

I wasn't expecting the professor to look the way he did, thinking he would be some grayhaired old guy dressed in a white lab coat. Was I in for a surprise! He had a lot of blazing red hair peeking out from under a bright green beret. His eyes were piercing blue and peered at us through the thickest pair of glasses I had ever seen. They were even thicker than Bob's. He was wearing a pair of yellow and blue plaid pants.

"Come in, children, come in," he said, in a high-pitched, off-key voice.

We went in, Bob pushing me ahead of him.

"And who is your young friend?" inquired the professor.

"This is my cousin Jessica, Professor," Bob said and stared at me until I put my hand out to shake the small pale hand. "How do you do, Professor?" I stammered.

"I do just fine, thank you," was his squeaky answer.

"Now, sit down, you two, and tell me about your discovery," the professor chirped.

I looked around but could not see any place to sit. There was junk and bits and pieces of stuff all over the room. There were also about eight cats in the room lying around on chairs, on the floor and on the window ledges.

"Now here, get out of the way, Willy, let this nice young lady sit down," he commanded shrilly as he shooed a huge Siamese off one of the chairs. Reluctantly, the big cat jumped off the chair, disappearing into another room.

Finally, we were able to sit down, and we began to tell him about the bugs on the other side of the island. He listened with much interest, all the while tapping his finger on the side of his cheek.

When we finished, he said, "You must take me to this spot as soon as possible. I need to see for myself. Although not an entomologist, I know a few things about insects and may be able to identify them."

Just then, one of the smaller cats jumped up

on my lap and began to purr. "Samantha likes you," the professor peeped. "She doesn't usually take to strangers."

The cat was sleek and coal- black. She purred all the louder when I petted her, then curled up on my lap for a sleep. "Would you like to have her?" asked the professor.

"Gee, I would love to, but I will have to ask my mom first," I said.

"Well, I guess we had better go," Bob said. He stood up, ready to leave

"You must have some of my herb tea first," the professor insisted. He bustled over to the stove to put the kettle on.

He was a very small man, probably not much over five feet tall, and he was very skinny. He looked like he had not eaten a good meal in a long time. I thought he resembled a leprechaun, but he had really large feet. I noticed that one of the soles on his shoe was loose, so it flip-flapped when he walked across the linoleum floor.

We talked as we drank what tasted like raspberry tea sweetened with honey. The professor gave us each a huge blueberry muffin that was scrumptious! I ate every scrap of mine. Then it was time to go. I was beginning to enjoy the visit. I thought the professor was pretty neat.

"I will let you know about the cat," I said as we went out the door. "Thank you for offering her to me. Cats are my favourite animal, but I have never had one of my own."

"Thanks for the tea and the muffin," Bob said as we were almost out of the door.

"Come back again the next time I visit the bakery," the professor laughed. "Now, you will take me out to your find first thing on Sunday morning, won't you?" the professor asked. "I am busy tomorrow, as there are some molds that have to be attended to."

"Yes, we can go right after church," Bob replied.

"Well then, you come by when you are ready, and we will all go," said the professor. "Good-bye for now you two." He waved that pale hand at us. Then he shut the door.

After we managed to find our way out of the yard, through the brush, I wanted to know everything about the professor. "What did he mean about molds?" I asked.

"I don't know for sure, but he has invented a whole lot of neat stuff," was Bob's answer.

"He is very weird, but he is nice and kind. The cats look like they are well taken care of. How does he make a living? How come no one ever sees him?" I said, all in one breath.

"He sells some of his inventions, and he really keeps to himself," Bob answered.

Bob's family had lived on the island a lot longer than mine had. In fact, he was born here. He knew more people than I did, that's for sure.

Mom was waiting for me when I got home. "Where were you?" she asked. "I was wondering why you weren't home. Marcie has been phoning every fifteen minutes looking for you.

"Margie tells me that you and Bob are up to some thing. She says you go somewhere almost every day after school. I know you went away somewhere on the weekend, both days as a matter of fact."

"Oh we were just riding our bikes around."

Aunt Margie was Mom's sister. She didn't work, so she was home all day. She knew pretty much what was going on.

"Well, if you are not going to tell me, it will be difficult to find out, but you are very mysterious these days," Mom remarked. "You had better phone Marcie. It sounded like it was really important."

Marcie invited me to go with her and her parents over to the big island to see a movie. Mom told me it was ok with her. I went with them, and we had a good time.

It was late when we got back. Mom was still up. She had hot chocolate ready. I told her about the new Star Wars movie we had seen. She didn't ask any more questions about where Bob and I had been.

I wondered if Billy had blabbed to Aunt Margie, but I really believed he was keeping quiet about it, or a lot of other people would know by now. Maybe he wasn't so bad after all. I decided to phone Bob in the morning to suggest that we include Billy in the trip with the professor, just to be on the safe side.

I had a good sleep that night, waking to the sound of robins outside my window about six a.m. It was too early to get up, so I turned over and went back to sleep until Mom tapped on my door. "Rise and shine, Jessica Lynne. It's after eight o'clock, and we have work to do."

The day went quickly. In no time supper was ready, then it was time for bed.

I woke early again next morning to get ready for church. Mom had breakfast all ready. "What are you going to do today?" she asked.

"I don't know, probably not much of anything, maybe go for a bike ride, and I have some homework to do," I lied.

"Make sure you get your homework done," she reminded me as we went out the door.

After church, I hurried home, got into my grubs, and called Bob. "I am all ready to go. Should we ask Billy if he wants to come? He has been pretty good about keeping the secret. We don't want to do anything to change that."

"Billy has gone into the city with my dad to buy a new bike. He didn't even say anything about going with us. Let's meet at the professor's place as soon as we can get there," he said.

I got to the professor's house at exactly twelve o'clock. Bob arrived a few minutes later. It was then that I remembered some thing. I had forgotten to ask Mom about the cat. It would be better to wait until I was back home to ask her or she would start with the questions.

Off we went. The professor, still dressed in the beret and the plaid pants, was riding an old mountain bike that looked like he had used parts from several bikes, putting them together to make this one. The important thing was that it did run. We were on the other side of the island in no time at all.

The spider-bugs had grown in that short time. They were more than twice the size they had been when we saw them last. The little creatures were lined up in a neat little row, almost like soldiers. When they saw us, they raised their antennae and started toward us. We stood there watching them. Suddenly, they scurried away as though we had frightened them.

"I must have a specimen," squawked the professor. He had brought some kind of a science kit along. He was examining the closest insect through a huge magnifying glass that made his eyeglasses look even bigger and thicker.

"Hmmm, very interesting," he was muttering in his screechy voice to no one in particular. Suddenly he reached down and quickly scooped one of the insects up in his hand, thrusting it into a jar. Then he closed the lid. "Aha, little fellow, I have you," he snorted.

The other insects quickly disappeared. They were nowhere to be seen.

"Show me the egg sac," the professor demanded. Bob pointed to it. It had shrunk to a very small size. The professor picked it up, put it into a plastic bag, then into his bicycle carrier.

"All right, let's be off," said the little man. "I want to get back to my lab right away to study this interesting creature."

As soon as we arrived back at the professor's

wee house, he sent us home, saying, "I must have time to study this insect by myself, and I will need time to think. There cannot be any distractions of any kind. You do understand, don't you?"

Disappointed, we agreed and went home. We were full of questions, but we knew we were going to have to wait until the professor decided to share his findings with us.

Bob and I went to his place, where we played Monopoly for a while, but neither of us enjoyed the game. We finally gave up and watched TV until it was suppertime.

In the excitement, Bob and I had missed our lunch. Aunt Margie invited Mom and me for supper. We ate early. I was starved. All through the meal, I kept glancing at Bob and Billy, trying not to talk about our find in the woods. They must have been doing the same thing. Mom, Auntie, and Uncle were talking about politics, which was not the least bit interesting.

After we finished eating, we all played Scrabble. It went better than the Monopoly game.

At nine o'clock, Mom said, "Are you ready to go home, Jess? We both have an early day tomorrow."

I was more than happy to go home, because I needed to sit and think on my own for a while. I was sure surprised that Billy was able to keep the secret. Bob must have really scared him about what might happen if he opened his mouth.

I remembered that I did have homework to do, so I had to sit down and get it done. It was difficult to concentrate, but finally it was finished. I went straight to bed. "See you in the morning, Mom," I said sleepily and trailed off to my room.

"Sleep tight, don't let the bedbugs bite," came her reply. Yikes! I didn't need to be reminded about what had been on my mind all day. Bugs!

The next morning dawned cloudy and rainy. Typical Monday! I dragged myself to school and got through the day.

Marcie asked me to go to the store with her. She needed to buy some things for school. "I haven't seen much of you this last week," she complained. "What have you been up to?"

"Oh nothing really, just busy with homework and stuff," I replied.

"Mom says I can have a sleepover next week and invite some of my friends. Can you come?"

she asked.

"Sure, love to, if it is ok with my mom," I answered. "Let me know when."

"It will likely be Saturday," she said. "Well, I have to get going. My mom is away this week, so that leaves me to cook supper for my dad and little sister. See you at school tomorrow," she called over her shoulder, as she turned the corner for home.

Chapter Four
Spiders Eh!

At home, the phone rang. It was Bob. "Did you hear from the professor?" I asked.

"No, and I know better than to disturb him when he is working," Bob answered.

"Well, we will just have to wait," I said, impatient to know what he had discovered.

Just then, Mom came home. She told me that she had received the divorce papers. She seemed relieved that it was all finally coming to an end. I was upset, but didn't say anything. Instead, I changed the subject and asked her if we could take the cat that the professor called Samantha.

She thought for a moment, then said, "I don't see why not, as long as you take good care of her and don't let her scratch the furniture."

"Gee, thanks, Mom!" I said, giving her a great big hug. "I will take perfect care of her. Just wait until you see her. She is so beautiful."

I phoned Bob again to tell him the good news. He said he hoped we would hear from the professor tomorrow.

The next day was Tuesday. I usually went to the library after school was dismissed. I had skipped last week, so I needed to go and get caught up on my reading. There were books to return anyway. After school I headed to the local library and proceeded to lose myself in the junior section.

In no time, my watch said five o'clock. I had to rush home to start supper. We were having leftovers anyway, so it wasn't going to be too much work.

I signed out three books that looked good, then left the library.

On the way home, I ran into Bob. He was out of breath and so excited he could hardly talk. He said, "I have been looking for you all over the place. The professor phoned and told me that he still doesn't know what the insect is, but he is getting closer to finding out. He wants us to come over tomorrow after school. He will probably have more to tell us then. He also said that if you still want the cat, you could take her tomorrow."

"Is that all he said?" I asked, crankily. "Doesn't he know any more than that?"

"I guess not," Bob answered. You could tell

that he was just as anxious as I was to find out about our bugs, probably even more.

I wondered if the professor was really as smart as Bob believed. Well, tomorrow might give us the answer.

I walked in the door to find Mom on the phone. When she saw me, she sort of lowered her voice. I couldn't hear what she was saying. Strange, she usually did not try to keep her conversations that private. I went to my room to give her some space.

In a few minutes, there was a tap on my door. It was Mom asking me to come out to help her with supper. She did not say a word about the telephone call, and I wasn't going to pry.

Next morning at school, l asked Bob if he had heard from the professor again, but he said he hadn't. All he knew was that we were supposed to go to the professor's house after school, Bob said he was bringing Billy with him.

Samantha was out in the yard. She came right up to me, purring and rubbing her back against my leg. I picked her up and stuck my nose into her soft black fur. No doubt about it, I was hooked on this cat.

No one answered our knock. The door was wide open, so we went inside.

The professor was nowhere in sight. Bob led us through the house into what looked like a laboratory or workshop. The professor was wearing the green beret, plus he had on a pair of bright orange coveralls. They looked really wild with his red hair. This must be his working outfit!

"Well, well, you two, you have brought a new face today. "Who is this smart-looking young man?" he asked, while peering at Billy over the top of his glasses. Bob introduced his little brother.

The professor invited us all to come over to the worktable where he was studying the body of the insect. "I have not been able to identify this creature," he said. "It has characteristics of an arachnid, but it certainly has unusual features. It has antennae, and it is hard shelled like a beetle." His face became very serious at this point. "Now, the strangest thing of all is that this creature is made completely of metal. Not only that, it is a metal unknown to this world. However, I can assure you it was once as alive as any one of us standing here at this table."

Billy looked completely shocked. Bob looked fascinated, and I felt confused. Wow! Was this ever something! I sure started to think about what this might mean.

The professor's face darkened, then he said, "We must not speak of this to anyone. To do so would cause a disturbance of great proportions on this island. You all know what that would mean. We would be overrun with scientists, curiosity seekers, plus news reporters and their kind."

"But do you think these things mean us harm? Shouldn't we tell someone about them? We don't know what might happen," Bob interrupted.

"Yes, what you say is quite true. We do not know what we are dealing with. They are not of this earth. But if I can find a way to destroy them, no one need know they were ever here," the professor replied patiently.

"I cannot help but think they were sent here deliberately," I said.

"That may very well be," came the professor's answer, "but we have no way of knowing who sent them, or where they originated from. They may have evil intent. I say we get rid of them as soon as possible."

Bob's brows furrowed, deep in thought. "The professor is right, Jess," he said finally. "We don't know for sure what might happen if word got out. The government might send in the army and our little island would never be the same again."

I shuddered at that thought. "What do you plan to do, Professor?" I asked.

"Well, I am not sure yet, but there must be some way of creating an enemy to eliminate them," he answered. He was tapping the side of his cheek again. His face was like a mask.

Suddenly, he stood up and announced that he was going back to the site again the next day. We could all come along if we wanted.

Billy, face as white as a ghost, hadn't said a word at all. Finally, he blurted out, "Not me, I am never going near those things again. They are too weird for me."

"How about you two?" the professor asked, his piercing look fixed on Bob and then on me.

"I guess you c-c-can c-c-count us in, r-r-right, Jess?" stammered Bob.

"I-I g-g-guess so," I managed to answer. My throat was dry and I felt scared stiff. The idea of having to meet those metal monsters again did not sound like a fun thing.

"We must act quickly. It is strange that no one has seen them except us," said the professor. "It's because it has been so wet and cool this spring," Bob replied. "No one is out walking very much, and the bugs are sort of hidden in a bushy area."

"Mom says I can take Samantha," I said, anxious to change the subject. "Thank you very much for giving her to me. I promise to take very good care of her. You can come and visit her if you like."

The professor smiled a rare smile, then answered, "Yes, I would like that. You know I get rather lonely here, even with all my cats. Samantha, that little black mouser, will be missed. She is the best hunter of them all. Now, you'd best get going. I will call you tomorrow."

Chapter Five
The Professor's Plan

We left the professor's house like we were all in a trance. No one said a word.

I carried Samantha in my arms. She didn't move a muscle. I left my bike at the professor's. I would have to go back for it.

When we got as far as my house, Bob finally spoke. "We really have found a problem, Jess. Do you think the professor is right? He made the decision. We will not tell anyone else about it, and we will try to solve this problem on our own?"

"Let's hope so," I remarked doubtfully. I was nervous about all this, yet didn't want the whole world invading our little island and turning it into a circus.

"See you tomorrow," Bob shouted as he hurried down the street, his little brother close on his heels.

Mom was home. She made a big fuss over the cat. "First thing we have to do is buy some cat food. Do we need some cat litter too?" she asked.

"I don't think so. The professor has about eight of them. He probably doesn't use cat litter for that bunch. Maybe we should get some though, because we are both away all day."

"Let's go then," said Mom.

In a second, we were in the car, cat and all. Samantha rather enjoyed the ride to the grocery store. She didn't freak out once.

"While we are out, let's get a pizza," Mom suggested. We stopped at the only place in town and ordered a big Supreme, then rushed it home.

It was piping hot. We found out that the new member of the household liked pizza too. Samantha was right in there when the box was opened. She persisted until we gave her some. "I like this cat already," Mom said. "She knows what she wants and won't give up until she gets it."

Samantha slept at the foot of my bed all night. We decided to keep her in the house for a few days until she became used to us. When I left for school, she was sitting in the window, making little growling noises at the birds outside.

School was a little more exciting that day. Tyler Small brought his pet white rat to school for everyone to see. It somehow got out of the cage after lunch and was loose in the classroom. I was sure that creep Trenton Farnov had deliberately let him out, because he looked so smug with a smirk on his face right after it happened. Most of the girls were freaked and would not go into the room. The boys were having a great time telling them that they had seen it in various people's desks. The idea of running into a rat face to face wasn't great, but at least I wasn't hysterical like some of the girls.

I told Trenton that he had let the rat loose deliberately. He smiled a toothy smile, then said, "What makes you think so, Shorty?"

I saw red! Before I realized, I had punched him right in the eye and kicked him in the shin.

Miss Bowman came over, separated us, and guided me to the principal's office for a short discussion. He gave me a lecture and a detention. It was worth it though. No one was going to get away with calling me Shorty. My detention was only half an hour. I could handle that.

Bob told me later that the rat, which Tyler had given the original name of Whitey, was finally found hiding behind a waste paper basket where no one, in all the confusion, had thought of looking. Whitey was placed back in his cage, and finally everything got back to normal.

By this time, it was nearly two thirty. Miss Bowman dismissed the class at that time. She said we might as well forget getting anything else done that day.

Bob and I were happy about getting out early, but with my detention, we were a little late. This was not a good day! We hurried home to get changed and rushed over to the professor's.

He was waiting outside for us. He was in a big hurry because he jumped on his old bike and took off as soon as he saw us, expecting us to follow. He hadn't said a word. We had a hard time keeping up with him.

We got to the woods in record time. The professor was off his bike, into the clump of trees like a jack-rabbit. Bob and I followed along as best we could.

I could not see the spiders, but the professor spotted them quickly enough. "Here they are," he shouted.

I looked more closely, and sure enough, they were there. The creatures had grown larger. They started moving out of our way quickly, clustering together, then quickly disappearing into the bush The only way you could describe their behaviour was as though they thought we meant them harm. I wondered how large they would grow. They were at least ten centimeters in length now. Their bodies were greenish and metallic-looking. The antennae were long and twitching as though there was some kind of communication going on among them. I shivered and stayed close to Bob and the professor.

"Remarkable, remarkable," the professor kept saying.

"What do you think we should do?" Bob asked him. "I am thinking of something, but cannot be sure of my strategy yet," the professor replied. "I will tell you when things are more clear in my mind. Then we will know how to proceed. In the meantime, please give me complete peace and quiet to formulate my plan. I would ask that you and Jessica make a regular trip over here to ensure that things are under control and no one has discovered them. Do you think you can do that?"

"I guess we can," Bob answered. He really sounded unsure of himself. He looked at me helplessly. Not feeling very sure of myself either. I just shrugged and nodded my head in agreement.

We left the clump of trees and started for home. Anxious about these alien spiders and the fact that we were not doing anything about them, I whispered to Bob, "Do you think he knows what he is doing?"

Bob whispered back, "I sure hope so. We have to trust someone. We got ourselves into this, so we can't blame anyone else."

The professor hopped off his bike when we got to his house. He told us that we should check on the spiders the next day and report back to him. He said he was going to start working on a solution to the problem. He suggested that he might need our help. That was all he said before he disappeared into the darkness of the house behind the thick brush.

The next couple of days went by quickly. Every day, Bob and I biked to the other side of the island to see what was happening to the spider creatures. Our spiders continued to grow. They seemed to be increasing in intelligence. The insects moved unbelievably fast. They seldom remained near us for more than a few seconds before they scuttled off together, antennae waving. Perhaps they felt safer in a group. At least that's what it looked like to me.

Marcie phoned me Friday evening to remind me that the sleepover would be on Saturday. She asked if I still wanted to come. She had invited two other girls, so it would be cool. Mom had already said it was ok with her. She would take care of Samantha.

Bob and I went back to check on our spiders on Saturday morning. We could not see them. Suddenly we spotted one at the edge of the trees. It was acting like a sentry or a lookout. When we got closer, it stood up on what looked like its hind legs as if prepared to do battle. I would have laughed if I hadn't been so scared. We did not go any closer. As a matter of fact, we backed away. We could see that it had grown some more. It was now more than fifteen centimeters in length, with a thick body.

"The professor had better find some way of getting rid of these things in a hurry," I said. "They are going to take us over if something isn't done soon." I was joking, but somehow it didn't sound like a joke. Maybe that was exactly what was going to happen.

Bob looked grim. He didn't say a word. He must have been thinking the same as me.

I went to Marcie's sleepover but wasn't feeling too happy.

The one thing I didn't like about Marcie was that she was always bragging. We have a new thirty-six-inch TV or we have a new car. It was always something. Tonight it was a new ice cream maker. We all made ice cream, and we had a great time doing it. I started to feel better and forget about the alien creatures in the woods.

The other two girls who were there, Annabelle and Sylvia, were full of fun. We had a lot of laughs watching videos and telling scary stories.

Then it was time to eat the ice cream. Smooth and creamy sweet with bits of chocolate and pecans mixed in, it was to die for. Between the bunch of us, we ate most of it.

By this time, it was nearly midnight. We could all see that Mr. and Mrs. Dean were tired. There was no way anyone in that house would get any sleep until the noise and laughter quieted down. They told us to call it a night, so we finally got settled and went to sleep.

I had been just itching to tell some one about the spiders in the woods, but I knew it was forbidden, so I decided to clam up about them.

I don't know what time we got to sleep, but I didn't hear a thing until Sylvia poked me in the ribs and said, "Wake up, sleepyhead. We are going to have ice cream for breakfast. It's after nine o'clock."

"Ugh! don't even mention the word ice cream for at least a week," I said.

We went down to the kitchen. I was thankful to see that Marcie's mom had made a nice normal breakfast for us.

After we ate, we played a few games of Nintendo. We had a lot of fun doing that. Then everyone had to go home. I thanked Marcie and her mom for the good time, said good-bye to the others and went home.

Mom and Samantha were waiting for me at the door. Mom asked me if I had enjoyed the sleepover. She told me there was a message from Bob to call him right away.

I tried to call, but he wasn't home. "What time did he call?" I asked.

"Oh, it was about ten," Mom answered. It was eleven thirty now. I had better wait around until Bob called back.

Bob called again about two thirty. I was helping Mom with the laundry. "Where were you when I called?" he asked.

"I was over at Marcie's. You knew she was having a sleep over," I said.

"I forgot, because the professor has kept me so busy helping him. We wanted you to go check on the insects," he was almost shouting! I never heard Bob sound so excited.

"What? me? By myself? Not likely," I was quick to answer.

"The professor and I are making something. You had better come over to his place and see for yourself," he said very quickly, then hung up.

"Where are you going, Jess?" Mom asked as I went out the door.

"Chores are all done, Mom." Hoping she wouldn't ask why, I said, "I am going over to the professor's house.

"Why don't you ask him to supper?" Mom suggested. "Mary Inglis is coming, so one more would not make a difference."

I breathed a sigh of relief. Thank goodness, at least there would be someone else to keep the conversation going. "Do you want me to call you and let you know if he can come?" I asked.

"No, just tell him to be here by five." she said and closed the door behind me.

In such a hurry, thinking so hard about what the professor and Bob were doing, I nearly got run down by a car. "Better be more careful, girl!" the driver yelled at me.

"Yikes, I'd better watch what I am doing!"

I just went in the house after knocking. No one would answer the door anyway I thought.

It took a few seconds for my eyes to adjust to the darkness in the room. There were no lights on. The cats were spread out all over the place. I made my way to the lab.

The lights were very bright in the lab. Bob and Professor Ipswich were busy at a big table. The professor was hammering something that looked like sheets of metal. Bob was wearing huge goggles, a pair of big heavy gloves, and using a torch on some of the metal pieces. I didn't have a clue what they were doing. It was very noisy.

I had to raise my voice to make them hear me. "What are you doing?" I shouted at the top of my lungs.

"We are creating some birds," the professor answered, as if that was the most natural thing in the world for people to be doing.

"Creating birds?" I said, surprised, unable to say anything else.

"Yes," the professor replied. "We will use these birds to destroy the insects."

They had both stopped working. The two of them stood there looking at me like I was some kind of an idiot for not completely understanding what was going on.

"You have lost me. I am not sure whether it

would help me to know what is going on anyway," I said. "You are both crazy."

"Well, it is really very simple," the professor explained. "We create birds made of metal, and they eat the spiders made of metal. End of story! Then, we do not have to worry about what those creatures are up to on this planet where they do not belong. The spiders possess a considerable amount of intelligence from what I have determined. There is no way we could capture them. However, the birds will be equipped with tracking devices which will seek them out, thus eliminating them."

"It all sounds goofy to me," I said. "But then what do I know?"

"Utmost secrecy is the key to our success," the professor whispered in his whiny voice.

"I would not breathe a word," I said. "Besides, every one would think I was out of my mind anyway. Professor, my mother wants you to come for dinner this evening about five o'clock. You're included too, Bob." I said.

"Well, thank you, I do accept," replied the professor.

"Thanks anyway," said Bob, "but we have been invited to dinner by the Hawkes." Bob looked a little disappointed.

"Well then, let us finish up here, young man. We can resume our work tomorrow," the professor announced.

I hurried home to let Mom know that the professor had accepted the invitation and to help her with supper.

Mom was just coming in the door. She looked really happy. I asked her what she was so pleased about, but she sort of ignored what I had said. She wanted to know if the professor was going to be with us for dinner, then warned me that we'd better hurry, because five o'clock was not far off.

Ms. Inglis arrived first. Mom told her that the professor had been invited for dinner. She looked a little shocked, but all she said was, "I have seen him in the library. He is very quiet isn't he?"

Oh great, I thought. That's all we need, two quiet ones at the same dinner table. I would have to do a lot of talking, and all I wanted to do was think about the latest developments in the spider situation.

When the professor arrived, he was wearing what looked like an old brown suit that must have belonged to someone twice his size. It was too long in the sleeves, and the pants were pretty long too. It looked clean and neat though. He had put some goopy stuff on his red hair to keep it from standing up all over the place. Actually, he looked quite good.

In his hand, he had a bouquet of daisies, which he handed to Mom. She asked him what his first name was. He told her it was Harold. So now we knew his first name.

He took my mother's hand, practically shaking it off her arm.

Mom introduced him to Ms. Inglis, only she called her Mary. Mary's face went beet red, right to the roots of her hair. She sort of stammered a hello to him. Oh wow! This is going to be some dinner!

Actually, dinner went very well, after everyone got settled down, the professor and Mary chatted away like they were old buddies. They talked about birds, butterflies, and the state of the world. Mom and I didn't have to make much conversation at all.

The professor spotted Samantha. He told me he thought I was taking good care of her, because she looked very contented.

When it was time for them to leave, the professor asked Mary if he could have the honour of walking her to her home. Again her face flushed, but she answered shyly, "Yes."

After they were gone, I said to Mom, "Wow, those two really got on well! The evening was great! You are such a wonderful person!" Then I gave her a big hug. Mom just smiled and, looking a bit sly, said, "I hope you don't think this is an attempt at trying to be a matchmaker, Jess. The thought never occurred to me until you spoke about how well they got on."

"I will never tell," I answered.

Chapter Six
The Plan is Carried Out

The next morning, Bob was at my door, waiting for me. We walked to school together. He sounded very serious. He wanted to know if I was going to go along with the professor's plan to get rid of the spiders. "You didn't seem convinced that it was a good idea. I wasn't sure what to think," he said.

"It's crazy, but if you and the professor both believe it will work, then who am I to disagree, besides, what choice do we have?" I replied.

Bob looked relieved and said, "I will continue to help the professor build the birds then. We really have to hurry because those spiders are getting bigger and stronger all the time."

Bob asked me to go with him to the professor's after school to see how the creation of the birds was coming along. Professor Ipswich was working like a beaver. He didn't notice us come in, but finally he looked up from his work and said, "Will you help too, Jess? We do not have much time. I was out to the woods today. These creatures are very organized. They knew I was coming before I got there. They formed a circle around me, but when I moved toward one of them, it backed away. Then they all scurried into the trees. It appeared like they had used some kind of signal. Perhaps they were testing to see how strong I was."

"What do you want me to do?" I asked.

"Perhaps you could help Bob assemble the birds while I put the sensor devices in them," he answered.

"How many are there?" I asked Bob.

"There are four. The professor believes that's enough to track down the spiders, then get rid of them," was Bob's answer.

We started putting the things together. It was like some kind of science project, only a lot creepier. They were made entirely of metal. The best way you could describe them was that they looked like storks, about one meter tall, with great long bills and legs. They did not have feathers of course, but long sheets of bronze-coloured metal made up the biggest part of their bodies. The legs and bills were dark, and there were metal hoods where the heads should be. They had three claws on each foot. They didn't have eyes, which made them even more weird.

We followed all the directions that the professor gave us. Finally it was done. The strange, sightless creatures stood silently in a row. The professor took them, one by one, and proceeded to install some sort of sensing device in it. This resulted in each bird now having a dim red light in the centre of the hood, which looked almost like a primitive eye. Boy! Were they ever queer looking!

The professor stood back, admiring our handiwork, then he said, "This ought to do the trick. All I have to do is activate them, and they will do the job intended. In each of my birds, I have implanted the scent from the dead spider. This will ensure that the other spiders will be tracked down and eliminated."

"Why do you think the spider that you caught died?" asked Bob.

"I believe it was primarily due to shock," the professor replied. "It was fortunate that I was able to capture one when I did, because they are now much too wary to be trapped that way. They only look very similar to our common spiders but are completely alien in their substance."

"How do you plan to get the birds to the

site?" I asked.

The professor did not seem concerned at all. "I have a friend that owns a pick-up truck," he answered. "Ray will let me use it for the day."

"Oh bother, you two have school tomorrow. That means we cannot go until after two thirty. I suppose we can get the job done in that time. Hopefully no one will be walking around in the woods, or our plan will be ruined."

The next day couldn't go fast enough to suit me. I was on pins and needles all day.

Trenton Farnov had a big black eye. He scowled at me all through classes, but I ignored him.

Finally, school was over, and we were on our way to the professor's to get the job done.

I asked Bob if Billy had talked to him about the spiders recently. He told me that Billy never mentioned them, and he didn't either. "Billy really got scared," I said. "After all, he is only seven, just a little kid. But what I cannot understand is why he has kept this whole thing a secret. I can't believe it."

"We will probably never be able to explain that," answered Bob. He looked a little funny, but I didn't ask any more questions.

Ray's pick-up truck looked like something out of the dark ages. It was rusted, and it rattled and shook something awful. In my mind was a question. Would it get us there?

"Hurry up, children," the professor urged. "We don't have much time. I have already loaded our brave birds on board." I sure hoped this plan would work, because what other tricks might he have up his sleeve?

The truck got us to our destination, groaning, snorting and creaking all the way. Bob and the professor unloaded the prehistoric type birds from the box of the truck. They stood in the grass on their long legs, looking very stupid and useless. There was no sign of the spiders.

The professor used some type of remote control, and the goofy birds started to move. They moved surprisingly fast too. In no time they were in the trees. You could hear them clicking and squeaking as they went about their task of gobbling up the alien spiders. I could see through the trees that the weird birds were zeroing in on the creatures, making quick work of them.

In a few minutes, the professor signaled his queer birds to come back. As soon as they were assembled in front of him, he turned off the remote, and they stood mute and dull once again. The professor flushed with pride at his achievement.

"There now, what do you think of that?" he beamed.

"Right on," said Bob. "I knew you could come up with a solution. Do you think they got them all?"

"I counted twenty-four the first day we were out here," the professor replied. "That was before they became so wary. That was probably all of them. I will wait two or three days before I melt the robot birds down, just to make sure. Can you and Jess come out over the next few days and check to see if there are any spiders remaining?"

"Yes, I think we can," Bob replied. "Ok with you, Jess?"

"Ok with me for sure," I answered quickly. I was in some hurry to make sure that these things were gone.

Bob and the professor tossed the birds into the truck box. We started off in the old truck, rattling and chugging along.

As soon as we got out to the main road, one of the birds bounced out of the truck, onto the road, right in front of a car that was following awfully close. The professor stopped the truck and jumped out so fast I couldn't believe he could move that quickly. He threw the bird back into the box, just as old Mrs. Pearkes got out of her car.

"Oh my goodness," dithered Mrs. P. "Is that alive? Did I run over it?"

"No, no," soothed the professor as he took her arm and gently assisted her back into her car. "It is perfectly all right, just an experiment I am conducting. No harm done. There is nothing for you to worry about, my dear."

In a moment, the professor was back in the truck and we were on our way.

"Close call," Bob murmured in my ear.

"It's a good thing it wasn't nosy old Mrs. Carver," I shouted over the noise of the truck. "By now she would be on her way to Main Street telling every one about this."

We arrived at the professor's house with no more mishaps. Bob and the professor unloaded the birds from the truck and put them in the lab. They looked completely harmless once again.

"I'd better get home," I said. "Mom will be waiting for me."

Chapter Seven
A New Twist

Mom had supper all ready when I got home.

"Gee, I am glad you are here," she said. "Jack Robbins has asked me to go to a concert with him over on the big island. He will pick me up at six thirty. Aunt Margie is coming over to keep you company."

"Mom, I don't need a baby-sitter," I objected.

"Well, it is best, after all, you are only eleven," she answered. "I insist. It will make me feel better to have someone here with you."

Oh horrors, Jack Robbins. There was no way to face him. Bob and I had made such fools of ourselves when we had called the cops on him. Besides, what was my mom doing anyway? Going out? I couldn't believe that. Worst of all, why was she choosing Jack Robbins?

My supper got gobbled up as fast as possible. Aunt Margie arrived, and I made some excuse about homework, disappearing into my bedroom just as Mr. Robbins pulled into the driveway.

After they left, I came back out to talk to my aunt. She was curious about what Bob and I had been up to. I was able to change the subject, so I didn't tell her much. Finally, we turned on the TV.

Mr. Robbins did not come in after he brought Mom home. Thank goodness! He drove Aunt Margie home. Mom shooed me off to bed.

The next morning, Mom told me what a good time she had and how much she enjoyed the concert. "Jack is good company. We have been out for coffee a few times. I would like to invite him to supper some time, Jess. Are you ok with that?" she asked.

If only she knew what his opinion was of me, I thought. "I suppose it is ok, after all, it is your house," I answered, not excited about the idea.

"Don't be cheeky, Jess," she snapped, taking me by surprise. "Is there something that you don't like about him?"

I blurted out the whole story. She laughed and said not to worry. Jack had told her about it. He said that after the initial shock, he had considered it funny.

I decided to let her know my real feelings. "Mom, why are you doing this? After all, you are not even divorced yet."

"Jess, be reasonable, I am only inviting him to dinner," Mom answered impatiently.

"How about if you invite him to dinner but tell him your daughter is sick with the flu," I suggested. Mom just raised her eyebrows at that.

It seems I hadn't been paying much attention to what was going on around home, being so busy with the spider thing. I didn't even realize that Mom knew Mr. Robbins.

I was angry walking to school. I kicked a stone that made my big toe throb for several minutes. That didn't help at all.

Lost in my thoughts, I walked right past Bob, who was waiting at the school entrance for me. "Whoa, wait up there," he said. "Are you on another planet?"

"What do you want?" I barked at him.

"Wow! Did you get out on the wrong side of the bed this morning or did someone pour gasoline in your corn flakes?" he teased.

I had to laugh at his remark, and my bad mood passed. The whole problem was my fear of losing Mom to some one else. That was it.

"Are we going to check on the spider population this afternoon?" Bob asked.

"Yes, we should," I answered.

Just then the school buzzer went. "See you at three at your place," he said.

We got out to the woods about three thirty. There was a lady walking her dog on the beach. She didn't even look our way as we dropped our bikes and went racing into the trees. We took a good look around, but didn't see any of the strange spiders. "Do you think they are all gone? Bob asked.

"Boy, all we can do is hope," I said. "This has sure messed up our lives," I complained.

"You are not telling me everything," Bob pried. "I know you. Something is bothering you."

Bob was my best friend, even if he was a boy and my cousin. He knew me better than any one. "Mom is dating Mr. Robbins," I said.

"Yikes! That's not cool," was his reply.

"Mom says he thinks what we did to him is funny. But do you believe that?" I asked.

"No, I don't," said Bob. "After all the trouble we caused him."

"Why should Mom be so interested in him?" I complained.

Mr. Robbins was a pharmacist. He owned the only drug store on the island. One evening, Bob and I had seen him trying to get in to the back door of the bank. We called the police. Guns drawn, they approached the poor man and handcuffed him, then took him into the station for questioning. As it turned out, he had an appointment with the bank manager, who had forgotten about it. He had not responded when Mr. Robbins came to the front door, so Mr. R. went to the back door, thinking he could get the man's attention.

"Well, there isn't much you can do," Bob said. "Just be happy for your mom if they are having a good time."

"I suppose you are right," I answered. "How can I face him though? Maybe he will move away somewhere. That would be good."

"Let's get out of here," Bob suggested. With that, we hopped on our bikes and sped for home.

Mom was waiting at the door for me. "I just can't figure out what you two are up to," she commented as I put my bike away. "Come in now," she said, "I have some good news."

Inside the house, she made me sit down. She went on to tell me that her boss had told her today that business was picking up. There would be no lay-off.

"That's great, Mom. You must feel better."

"He also told me that I could probably count on a raise in the summer if the business keeps growing," she continued.

"That is good news!" I said, giving her a quick hug.

The next day, Bob and I went back out into the woods to check on things. There was still no sign of any insects. "So far so good," I said.

Bob interrupted, "They might be hiding somewhere and we can't see them, but I don't know what else to do."

"There is no sign at all that there are any here," I said as we left the woods and headed back home. "I am sure that the birds got them all. After all, the professor's crazy birds wouldn't have missed any, because he put a sensor in each of them. At least that's what he said," I snapped at Bob, cross with him for being so uncertain.

We decided that Bob would report to the professor and tell him that we would make one more search of the area, then he could melt down the birds. He was not at home. We weren't too sure where to look for him.

Bob suggested we go the Burger Barn for a coke. "Do you have any money, Jess?" he asked.

"No problem," I said. Let's go."

At the Burger Barn, who should we see but the professor and Miss Inglis sitting together in deep conversation over milk shakes? We walked over to the other side of the restaurant to sit down.

"What do you make of that?" Bob asked. I shook my head and giggled. I told Bob about the dinner at my house and how well the two of them got on.

We finished our cokes and left. The professor and his companion didn't even look up "I'll phone him tonight," Bob said as we parted

Mom said she was going to invite Mr. Robbins over for dinner in a couple of weeks. She was trying to prepare me. It was impossible to get out of it. I had to face him sooner or later. Mom could see that I wasn't too happy about it. "Don't worry, sweetie," she said. "Jack has gotten over it, believe me." If she only knew how I really felt, but I couldn't tell her.

The next morning, Bob told me he had reported to the professor and told him that we would make one more trip into the woods before the birds were demolished. "Let's go today," he suggested.

"Fine with me," I answered. I felt quite sure

that there would be no spiders, and we could forget about the whole thing.

Was I in for a surprise! When we arrived at the edge of the woods that rainy afternoon, we saw something among the trees. We approached the thing, whatever it was. It looked like a small weather balloon. It was yellow in colour, with a long string attached. Connected to the string was a small pouch made of strange stuff. It occurred to me that Samantha would have a ball with it. It did not look dangerous, so I picked it up. It was as light as a feather. I wondered what had made it land.

"Should we open it?" I asked Bob. "We might as well," he replied. "Wait a minute, maybe we should take it to the professor," I said.

"If there is nothing inside it, then there is no point," was Bob's argument.

"I guess you are right," I agreed.

Bob opened the odd little pouch. It had very unusual markings with weird squiggles and lines all over it. It was an unusual green, the color of the ocean when there is a storm but the sun is still shining. "Hurry up," I urged Bob. His fingers seemed frozen, like he was afraid of what he might find inside.

Finally, he pulled out a piece of what looked

like thin brown paper. His hands were wet from the rain. He fumbled in his attempts to open the paper in front of him. I could see that there was writing on the page. Bob, wide-eyed by this time, handed me a sheet of funny-looking paper. I guess it was paper but I couldn't be sure. I stared at the writing. It was in a curious type of print. "Read it, Jess, my glasses are all covered with rain spots," Bob said.

I read aloud.

You have destroyed the Protectors. They were sent to your planet to act as your allies in the battle that the human race will soon be forced to wage. Instructions for the control of these creatures were in the hatching device. Had you followed these directions, you would have saved your world from the threat that is coming. We cannot aid you now. We are a friendly species from the planet Irintia. Our genus has watched over you for multiple centuries of your time. We are advanced beyond your weak civilization. The study of your system of communication has been done in depth; hence, our scribes are able to duplicate your language. We chose to send the Protectors to this island because we are aware of the plan of the enemy. The attack will occur in this area. If they gain control, they will take over the planet very easily from there. Beware the Sandalucian Walking Stick Menace. They have destroyed their own habitat and will destroy yours easily. Originally, they ate vegetation only. Due to natural mutation and the strong will to survive, they will devour every thing in their path.

We cannot help you now. You must defend yourselves with your own resources and ingenuity. There is very little time, as you know it, left.

That was the end of the note. Shaking like a leaf, I handed the bit of paper back to Bob. "Did I read what I think I just read?" I managed to speak in a choking whisper.

Bob's face was white as he read the note over again to himself. "I'm afraid you did," he replied. "It looks as though we have screwed up big time! What we have done is put the fate of the entire world in our hands, and we screwed up!" He held his head in his hands and shook it back and forth slowly, as if he could not believe what he had just seen.

"Perhaps it's all a joke," I said hopefully. "Maybe someone saw us out here getting rid of the spiders and decided to play a joke on us."

"Somehow, I don't think so," Bob answered. "We'd better get to the professor right away and ask him what we should do."

We hurried away on our bikes as fast as we could, directly to the professor's place. It looked like there was no one home when we got there. The front door was open ever so slightly. We knocked several times. The professor finally answered.

We were out of breath and could hardly talk. We both started babbling at once. "Slow down children, slow down," the professor soothed.

Bob was the one to tell the story. He told the professor about the note we had found inside the balloon and handed him the strange message. The professor turned pale as he read it.

Immediately, he went into the lab. We could hear him rummaging around in there. When he came back out, he was sweating, and his hands were trembling. He looked like he was about to collapse. "I destroyed the egg sac right after I came up with the idea of the birds. That would have been the proof that we needed to determine if the note is legitimate, and now we don't have that," he groaned.

He sat down, holding his head between his small pale hands, looking thoroughly beaten. "I am not sure what we should do," he said, "especially since we don't know how much time we have. First of all, we must alert the authorities, tell them everything."

"They may not believe us," I said. "It is pretty weird and hard to believe."

"We must make them believe us," the professor answered. "I made a mistake by not thinking the whole thing through before acting. That is unusual for me. I cannot for the life of me explain why I behaved that way. I melted the birds down this morning. Now this strange note is the only thing we have. It is certainly no proof of anything. I will phone the police first, They will know what to do."

He stood up and reached for the phone. We heard him talking to the police on the big island. Our police station had been closed since January. All he said was that some thing unusual had occurred and he needed to talk to them in person. He came away from the phone, looking a little relieved. "They will come here this evening at seven thirty," he declared. "You two

SPIDERS IN THE WOODS

must be here and bring your parents as well. There is no need for secrecy now. We are forced to make everyone aware of the peril that is about to befall us. I have no idea how to deal with it. Perhaps the army should have been contacted. Oh, I don't know. This makes me feel so responsible!"

"Don't think it's all your fault, professor," Bob answered. "Jess and I have to take some blame too. After all, we were the ones who found the egg. We should have looked in the egg sac then. I promise, Jess and I will be back tonight."

I was late getting home. Mom had that why-do-you-make-me-worry-look on her face.

I told her everything. She just stared at me and shook her head. "Jess, you really should try to control your imagination," she scolded. She didn't believe me! Somehow I knew that she wouldn't.

"Mom, that was the truth," I insisted. "Have I ever lied?"

"No you have not," she said. "But this game you and Bob have been playing, you actually believe that it is real?"

"Will you come with me to the professor's house tonight? The police are coming, and we need you to be there with us," I begged.

Mom, her shoulders sagging, sighed, "I thought you had learned your lesson after the incident with Jack, but I guess you haven't. I will go with you, but only to apologize to the police for your behavior. I cannot believe that this Professor Ipswich got so involved. People have said that he is strange. It should not be a surprise to me that he went along with you two. He probably believes in little green men from Mars too."

I was so upset. Dinner was awful! Not one word was said all through the meal. Mom was really put off with me. There was no way to convince her that we were telling the truth. I didn't know what else to say or do. Maybe the police would believe us. After all, they were the ones we had to convince.

Mom and I got to the professor's place just before the police did. Aunt Margie, Uncle Tim, Bob, and Billy were already there. Uncle Tim's face was dark and gloomy. There was not a sign of a smile on his face when we walked in. Billy and Bob both sat with their heads down, staring at their hands.

Professor Ipswich acted really nervous. He was sitting on the edge of his chair, fidgeting and tapping the side of his cheek.

Bob and I didn't look at each other. I faced the wall and studied the photos of two old people. They must have been the professor's relatives.

Two lady police officers arrived at exactly seven thirty. Their name badges said Constable McTavish and Constable Hunt. They took their hats off when they came in the door, but still looked awfully tall. Strangely enough, they both had red hair. The professor should feel right at home with them, I thought foolishly. They introduced themselves and accepted the professor's invitation to sit down. We all introduced ourselves, and the professor proceeded to tell the story.

The Officers listened politely, but it was evident that they did not believe a word. They kept glancing at each other all the while he spoke.

When the professor finished, Constable Hunt asked to see the note. She read it quickly and passed it on to the other officer. Constable McTavish stood up to what appeared to be a full six feet. She looked sternly at us and said, "Do you all realize that the perpetration of a hoax such as this can get you in a lot of trouble?"

"But Officer, we are telling you the truth," the professor implored.

Suddenly, Uncle Tim stood up. "I for one have heard enough of this nonsense," he growled. "Officers, I apologize for the behavior of these youngsters and for the fact that your time has been wasted. Come, Billy and Bob, we are going home. I will deal with you two tomorrow."

Redfaced and silent, the boys followed their mom and dad out the door.

The policewomen, both scowling, put their hats on and strode out of the door without saying another word.

Mom got up, frowned at me, then at the professor, and said, "Jessica, it is time for us to leave." To the professor, she said, " Harold, I am surprised that a man of your age and intelligence would be taken into a game as silly as this." Before he could answer, we were gone.

Mom drove the old car home very quickly, neither of us speaking. She looked at me sadly when we got inside the house and said, "Jess, I am not sure what to do with you. Perhaps the impact of what that police officer said was enough to sober you. You do realize that you could get in big trouble, don't you?"

"But Mom," I started to argue.

She turned and walked away, saying, "Jess, please go to your room. I am very angry and do not want to talk to you now."

I went to my room, sat, and stared at the walls until I fell over on the bed and went to sleep.

When I woke up the next morning, still fully dressed from the night before, my first thoughts were of what had happened yesterday. What was the Sandalucian Walking Stick Menace, and when was it coming?

I was so scared and felt so guilty about the whole thing, that my stomach was all upset. I had to run to the bathroom to throw up. Mom said that there was no way out of school that day. She was showing no mercy. I had a shower and changed, but I didn't feel any better.

I was late for class, only catching a glimpse of Bob. He sat in his seat, looking so glum you couldn't help but feel sorry for him. However, I felt more sorry for myself.

When the recess buzzer sounded, I got up to leave the room, but Marcie stopped me. She looked concerned and asked me what was wrong. "You look awful!" she said. I wasn't sure what to say. Not wanting to make a fool of myself again by telling her the truth, I told her it was a virus. She seemed satisfied with that and moved away rather quickly, as if she was afraid of catching some thing.

I caught up with Bob in the hallway. "My dad has grounded me for life," he groaned. "Besides, maybe life is going to be awfully short if those things from that other planet are as scary as the note said," he griped.

"When do you think we can expect them?" I asked. I didn't really want an answer, but I had to talk about the whole nightmare thing.

"It wasn't as if it was our fault," I said.

"But it was our fault," Bob reminded me. "If we had told someone else besides the professor, we might have had a chance of beating them. That was a crazy thing to do. Now we can't get anyone to believe us." I had to admit he was right.

"Is there anything at all we can do?" I asked Bob.

His answer was not encouraging. "Nothing I can think of except wait and see. Maybe, like you said, someone was playing a trick on us." He turned and walked back into the classroom, his shoulders slumped.

I was grounded too. Mom told me that

afternoon. She didn't say for how long, it was until further notice. I knew better than to ask any stupid questions.

I played with Samantha for a while. She wasn't very playful that day. It must have been my black mood.

Mom watched TV, and I tried to do some homework, but my effort wasn't very great. Finally, I went to bed and tried to sleep. My dreams were about some kind of monsters dropping from the sky.

Chapter Eight
The Sandalucian Walking Stick Menace

Each day seemed to fade into the next one. The weather was cool and wet.

I talked to Bob on the phone, but we were not allowed to get together at all. I was bored but also scared. Mom seemed to think I was feeling guilty over trying to pull off such a stunt. It made sense to let her think that, because there was no point in trying to convince her otherwise.

Mr. Robbins came to dinner. I already felt so awful that it didn't even bother me. He appeared concerned about me. I even began to think that maybe he was an ok guy.

It happened about ten days later. The teachers were having a professional day, so there was no school the whole day. It was just after two o'clock in the afternoon. The sky started to get dark, very fast, as if a really bad storm was about to happen, but it didn't actually look that stormy, because there were lots of patches of blue sky showing.

I ran outside to look. There were things flying out of the sky toward the ground. They were huge and a kind of a brown-green colour. They looked like some kind of monstrous insect, and they were really gross. I could see that they had huge beady black eyes and long spindly legs.

Was this the Sandalucian Walking Stick Menace that the Irintians had warned us about? There appeared to be thousands of them.

People started coming out of their houses to see what was going on. Every one of them looked terrified and started to shout at each other. "What are those things?" one woman screamed.

"They look frightful!" shrieked another.

One lady ran into her house and brought her husband out to see what was happening. He stared at the things with eyes like saucers. He ran inside pretty fast when they got closer. He was wearing a hair-piece. It tilted crazily to one side of his head. As frightened as I was, I started to laugh. I couldn't help myself. His wife shouted, "I am phoning the cops." She was right behind him, heading for shelter. About that time, I raced for my house too.

The ugly things began to land. Immediately, they started to eat grass, the leaves on the trees, even weeds, with huge chomping jaws. You could hear them munching their way through Mrs. Gagnons' hedge. Yikes! I thought. Would they start to chew their way into the houses next? What might happen then, humans for dessert? The Irintian message didn't exactly say that, but it didn't say they wouldn't either. The sky was black with the disgusting things.

All the people had gone inside their houses by this time. They were watching through the windows, peeking out from behind the curtains and blinds.

I was scared stiff! I grabbed Samantha and hung on to her, my heart pounding like mad.

The phone rang. It was Mom, who sounded scared too. She wanted to know if I was all right. She said she had heard some thing on the radio about some kind of huge insects falling out of the clouds, but she hadn't seen any yet. Then she let out a shriek, "I just saw one fly by the office window. Oh my goodness, what horrible-looking things! You stay put. Don't go anywhere until help arrives. The radio announcer said that he saw an army helicopter circling over the island."

Suddenly, in the sky overhead, I could see huge glistening strands of something that appeared out of nowhere. These strands or threads were spinning in the air and wrapping around the creatures, pulling them down. The creatures were trying to escape. Some of them did, but got caught up again in the sticky tough looking strands. It appeared to be a real struggle. The hideous insects were strong. They kept pushing against the tangle of threads they were caught in, but they weren't able to break free. Their long legs were getting caught up in the strange stuff. They were losing the battle.

Finally, the monstrous things were completely entangled, and it didn't look like any of these huge insects were able to escape. It seemed to me that this struggle went on for ages before all of the horrible things were caught in the webs. My Mickey Mouse watch said four o'clock.

The strands were sweeping in great circles, toward the other side of the island, dragging all the walking stick things with them.

I ran across the living room to my bedroom. The view was better out of that window. It looked as though the webs these things were caught in were being pulled toward the sea-shore. If they were dragged into the sea, would that drown them? I wondered.

A thought occurred to me, like a lightning bolt. Could those threads or strands be webs?

Were they spider webs?

It was impossible to see well enough from where I stood. Without thinking, I went outside, grabbed my bike and headed over to the other side of the island. There was no sign of the big ugly creatures in our yard or any of the neighbors' yards.

Close to the shore, I could see exactly what had happened. All of the insect-like things were in the sea.

Next thing I knew, Bob was beside me, out of breath, as he said, "Jess, some of the spiders survived. Isn't that wonderful?"

I shook my head, too stunned to talk. For once in my life, I couldn't say anything.

Bob shouted, "Can't you see, Jess, there are two spiders out on the ocean. Look at them!"

I struggled to see them against the glare. The sun had come out from behind the clouds. It was really bright, almost blinding. I put my hand up to shade my eyes and could just make them out. "They are enormous! They can swim too? What really awesome spiders we found!" I shouted.

"Those spiders, if that's what they are, saved us from those creepy things. They must have spun the webs that trapped the insects," Bob said in awe.

"I wonder how the spiders escaped the birds," Bob said.

"I don't know, but wow, is it ever great that they did!" I answered.

We ran down right to the water's edge. We could see even better from there. Some of the nasty-looking creatures had washed up on the shore onto the sand. They were dead but still looked frightening. They had huge beady black eyes, long pincers, stubby wings and long spindly legs.

Bob looked at them for a long time. He turned to me and said, "Jess, I think I know what these things are. They are Praying Mantis! No different than the Praying Mantis we learned about in school, except these are much larger."

"Right on," I said. That's what the Irintians meant when they warned us about The Sandalucian Walking Stick Menace. Aren't the Praying Mantis often called "The Walking Stick Insects" because of their long stick-like legs?"

"Yeah, I think that's true," Bob said.

I looked up at the sky. I could hear a low hum coming from above. "Can you hear that? I asked Bob.

"Yeah, I can," he replied. "What is it? It isn't

a helicopter. It isn't loud enough."

We didn't have to wait long for our answer. Hovering over the ocean was a huge silver saucer-shaped spacecraft. There were green and red lights flashing along the sides of it. It revolved around and around as it lowered itself closer and closer to the sea and to the spiders.

The spiders were suddenly swept up toward the craft and disappeared into it. In a flash, with a loud whoosh, the space ship took off and vanished before our eyes. It was so fast, I really wasn't sure what had actually happened.

"What was that, Bob?" I asked.

"It looked like a flying saucer," he answered. "And it took our spiders away."

It wasn't long before there were news people, government officials and the police, all over the island.

We did not see the two officers that interviewed us. I was happy about that.

Bob and I didn't say a word to anyone about the whole thing, except we did talk to Mom and his parents about it. We will never know if they truly believed our story, because no one would talk about it, but they lifted our grounding punishment, and Mom was really supernice to me after that.

The following day, Bob, Billy, and I went over to the other side of the island. We searched the woods from one end to the other. We found no trace of any remaining spiders. My guess was that the Irintians had come back to take them away, and that it was their space ship that came down. Who knows? I was so relieved to see that everything was back to normal, I didn't really want to find out.

I asked Billy how come he was able to keep the secret. It was killing me not to know. While Bob was looking for the spiders, he whispered to me, "Bob promised to give me part of his allowance, so I could buy a kite. I have always wanted one, but have never been able to save up enough of my own allowance." I knew Bob wasn't telling me the truth about Billy's silence but I had decided not to bug him about that.

The Walking Stick things were mostly all washed out to sea. The gulls were scoffing up the remaining ones

When all the excitement died down, Bob and I went to visit the professor. He was in good spirits, dressed in a bright pink and black checkered jacket and in the middle of a phone call to Mary Inglis. He waved at us cheerily. After he hung up the phone, he didn't want to talk about the recent occurrences on the island. All he would say was that he had made a grave mistake in not informing the authorities right off. He admitted that he was terribly relieved that everything turned out all right.

As for me, I still had to get my head around the fact that Mr. Robbins, I mean Jack, was ok. It looked like he would be a permanent fixture in our lives. If he was good for Mom, then he must be good for me. I would try hard to believe that.

Mom always told me that my imagination was too wild. For now, I was going to try to just be a normal kid and not get myself into any trouble.

I had a whole new attitude toward spiders too. I didn't hate them anymore. After all, it was our friendly alien spiders that had saved our planet.

*

Printed in the United States
6324

9 781591 295808